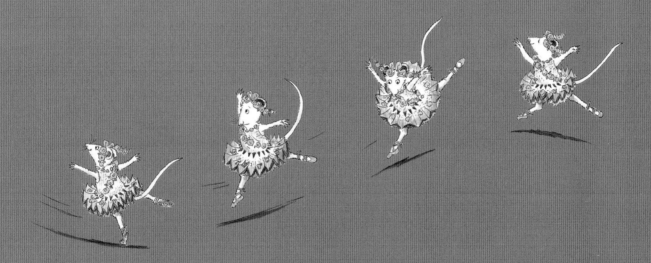

To my grandsons, Nat and Will. Also, love and thanks to my brother, John, for valuable advice   HC
To my mother, D. K. Holabird, and the Bateau St. Georges   KH

VIKING
Published by Penguin Group
Penguin Young Readers Group, 345 Hudson Street, New York, New York 10014, U.S.A.
Penguin Group (Canada), 90 Eglinton Avenue East, Suite 700, Toronto, Ontario, Canada M4P 2Y3 (a division of Pearson Penguin Canada Inc.)
Penguin Books Ltd, 80 Strand, London WC2R 0RL, England
Penguin Ireland, 25 St Stephen's Green, Dublin 2, Ireland (a division of Penguin Books Ltd)
Penguin Group (Australia), 250 Camberwell Road, Camberwell, Victoria 3124, Australia (a division of Pearson Australia Group Pty Ltd)
Penguin Books India Pvt Ltd, 11 Community Centre, Panchsheel Park, New Delhi – 110 017, India
Penguin Group (NZ), 67 Apollo Drive, Rosedale, North Shore 0632, New Zealand (a division of Pearson New Zealand Ltd.)
Penguin Books (South Africa) (Pty) Ltd, 24 Sturdee Avenue, Rosebank, Johannesburg 2196, South Africa

Penguin Books Ltd, Registered Offices: 80 Strand, London WC2R 0RL, England

Angelina Ballerina © 2004, 2008, Helen Craig Ltd. (illustrations) and Katharine Holabird (text).
The Angelina Ballerina name and character and the dancing Angelina logo are trademarks of HIT Entertainment Limited,
Katharine Holabird and Helen Craig Ltd. Reg. U.S. Pat. & Tm. Off.
All rights reserved

First published in Great Britain by Puffin Books, 2004
First published in the United States of America by Pleasant Company Publications, 2004
This edition published by Viking, a division of Penguin Young Readers Group, 2008

3 5 7 9 10 8 6 4

The Library of Congress has cataloged the Pleasant Company edition under LC Number 2004040116
This edition ISBN 978-0-670-01108-7

Manufactured in China
Set in Bembo

Angelina, Star of the Show

Story by Katharine Holabird   Illustrations by Helen Craig

VIKING

"Welcome aboard *The Jolly Rat*, Angelina," said Grandma and Grandpa. "Are you ready to set off for the Mouseland Dance Festival?"

"I can't wait," said Angelina. "I'm going to think up a special dance on the way, so I can be the star of the show! Do you like my costume?"

"It's lovely, but we need all paws on deck to get the boat to the festival," Grandpa reminded her as he started the engine.

But Angelina wasn't listening. She skipped around the deck, imagining her great performance.

"Aren't you going to wear your overalls?" asked Grandma, in surprise.

Angelina smiled sweetly and shook her head. "I've decided to stay in my costume," she said.

As *The Jolly Rat* chugged along through the countryside, Angelina twirled and danced, stopping only to pester her grandparents with questions.

"What do you think of this step?" Angelina asked, and "Does this look nice?"

"You're a sailor now," Grandma reminded her sternly, but Angelina was too busy dancing to be a sailor.

"*The Jolly Rat* needs a new coat of paint,"
Grandpa announced, and he handed
Angelina a paintbrush.

"But, Grandpa, I really *have* to practice. I've got a whole new
dance routine to think up!" said Angelina, and she spun
into Grandpa's can of paint and waltzed off, leaving
little footprints all over the deck!

After that, Grandpa decided Angelina should help Grandma
down in the galley. But Angelina forgot to watch the soup
while she practiced pliés, and it all boiled over.

That afternoon, Angelina worked on her arabesques, and it wasn't long before she got all tangled up in Grandma's clothesline and Grandpa's fishing line. She had to be rescued by both her grandparents, who were getting very grumpy. "That's enough, Angelina!" they cried.

When Angelina went
to bed that night, she promised
Grandma and Grandpa that she would
stop dancing. But the very next morning, Angelina forgot,
and performed a magnificent series of leaps along the deck.

The deck was slippery, and Angelina lost her balance.
She tumbled right into a can of oil and
got covered from head to toe in
horrible black grease.

"Oh no—look what I've done!"
Angelina gasped. Her beautiful costume was ruined.

Angelina was so horrified that she raced below deck to her bunk bed and cried her heart out. Then, just when she had decided she was the worst mouseling in the world, Grandma came to give her a cuddle.

"I'm sorry, Grandma!" Angelina sobbed. "I haven't been very helpful, have I?"

"I know you're sorry," said Grandma as she dried Angelina's tears.

"I haven't got anything to wear to the dance festival now," sniffed Angelina. "And I can't do my dance without a costume!"

"Well, let's see what's in my old trunk," suggested Grandma.
And there, inside the trunk, they found a beautiful sailor suit.

"That was my favorite outfit," Grandma said.
"And that's me wearing it," she added
proudly, pointing to a faded photograph
that was hanging on the wall.

"Ooh," gasped Angelina excitedly.
"Do you think I could borrow it
if I'm very careful?"

"Of course," smiled Grandma.
"I'll add some special ribbons."

For the rest of the journey, Angelina wore her old overalls, and she tried very hard to be a real sailor.

Before long, she could steer *The Jolly Rat* down the Mousetail Canal.

She swabbed the decks and painted the woodwork with Grandpa, and she cooked with Grandma down in the galley.

She even baked her grandparents some cheddar-cheese pies!

And in the evenings after supper, while Grandpa played his pennywhistle, Grandma showed Angelina some of her favorite dances.

"Thank you, Grandma," said Angelina one night. "You've given me a wonderful idea."

A few days later, *The Jolly Rat* arrived at the Mouseland Dance Festival
with a new coat of paint and all decked out in garlands of flowers.

Angelina proudly tooted the horn.
"We're here!" she shouted.

As the festival opened, Grandpa played his pennywhistle and Angelina performed her new dance. It was a special sailor's jig that she'd practiced with Grandma. The crowds loved the show and cheered for more.

"Hooray for the little sailor!" they shouted.

When the evening was over, Angelina hugged her grandparents.

"You really were the star of the show," said Grandma.

"And you're the very best grandma and grandpa in all of Mouseland!" Angelina replied.

Then they joined paws and skipped happily back to *The Jolly Rat*.